P

The R

Frank Rodgers has written and illustrated a wide range of books for children: picture books, story books, how-to-draw books and a novel for teenagers. His work for Puffin includes the highly popular *Intergalactic Kitchen* series and the picture books *The Bunk-Bed Bus* and *The Pirate and the Pig*, as well as the best-selling *Witch's Dog* titles. He was an art teacher for a number of years before becoming an author and illustrator. He lives in Glasgow with his wife and two children.

Some other books by Frank Rodgers

THE ROBODOG

THE ROBODOG AND THE BIG DIG

THE WITCH'S DOG

THE WITCH'S DOG AT
THE SCHOOL OF SPELLS

THE WITCH'S DOG AND THE MAGIC CAKE

THE WITCH'S DOG AND
THE CRYSTAL BALL

THE WITCH'S DOG AND THE
FLYING CARPET

THE INTERGALACTIC KITCHEN SINKS

Picture books

THE BUNK-BED BUS

THE PIRATE AND THE PIG

Frank Rodgers

The Robodog
Superhero

PUFFIN BOOKS

PUFFIN BOOKS

Published by the Penguin Group
Penguin Books Ltd, 80 Strand, London WC2R 0RL, England
Penguin Putnam Inc., 375 Hudson Street, New York, New York 10014, USA
Penguin Books Australia Ltd, 250 Camberwell Road, Camberwell,
Victoria 3124, Australia
Penguin Books Canada Ltd, 10 Alcorn Avenue, Toronto, Ontario, Canada M4V 3B2
Penguin Books India (P) Ltd, 11 Community Centre, Panchsheel Park,
New Delhi – 110 017, India
Penguin Books (NZ) Ltd, Cnr Rosedale and Airborne Roads, Albany,
Auckland, New Zealand
Penguin Books (South Africa) (Pty) Ltd, 24 Sturdee Avenue,
Rosebank 2196, South Africa

Penguin Books Ltd, Registered Offices: 80 Strand, London WC2R 0RL, England

www.penguin.com

First published 2002
3 5 7 9 10 8 6 4

Copyright © Frank Rodgers, 2002
All rights reserved

Set in Times New Roman Schoolbook

Printed in Hong Kong by Midas Printing Ltd

British Library Cataloguing in Publication Data
A CIP catalogue record for this book is available from the British Library

ISBN 0–141–31032–4

Chip, the robodog, was having
fun in the park with Gary and
Sue. He fetched sticks, played catch
and ran around among the trees.
But soon it was time to go home.

1

"Come on, Chip," Sue said. "We have to hurry. Mum is taking you to the robot display at the Town Hall this afternoon."

The robodog started to trot towards them. But just then some dogs ran into the park and began to play.

Chip's ears swung up.
He really wanted to
make friends with
the other dogs.

"Woof!" he barked, running
over to them.

His tinny, crackly bark stopped the
dogs in their tracks and they stared
at him in surprise.

The dogs sniffed Chip warily.

Chip thought they
would be
friendly …

but they weren't interested.
They turned, ran away and
began to play again.

The robodog watched them
wistfully. It would be wonderful
to have friends to play with.

"Chip!" called Sue
again. "Come on!"

Chip turned and joined them
at the gate.

Back in the garden, Gary took the robodog off the lead.

"We'll go and tell Mum we're back, Chip," he said.

Chip wandered across the grass and looked into the next-door garden. It belonged to snooty Mr and Mrs Minted.

He grinned. Rex, the Minteds'
Afghan hound, was there.

Chip liked Rex.
Perhaps Rex
could be
his friend?

"Woof!" he
barked and
trotted through
the gap in the
fence.

At that moment Mr and Mrs
Minted came out of the house.
"Oh! There's that walking computer
thingy from next door," said Mr
Minted. "What's it doing in our
garden?"

"Trying to be friends with Rex, by
the looks of it!" cried Mrs Minted in
annoyance.

"Go on, shoo!" she shouted, flapping her hands at Chip. "Leave our pedigree dog alone. I don't want him being friendly with the likes of you!"

"Yes, go on, scat!" smirked Mr Minted.

"You might give Rex a virus. A *computer* virus, ha ha!"

9

Mr and Mrs Minted snorted with
laughter as Chip turned and walked
sadly back to his own garden.

It looked like
he'd never find a
friend.

Mum met him in the garden. She
had heard what the Minteds had
said.

"Never mind," she said, stroking Chip's head.

"One day they'll find out just what a wonderful dog you are.

Now, come on," she continued, "let's check your computer systems before the display."

They went into the workshop and
Mum tested the robodog's wiring,
motors and sensors.

Finally, she cleaned off the mud
from the park and polished his
casing.

"There," she said,
satisfied. "You look as
bright as a button.
Let's go back to
the house."

Sue and Gary were in the living room. Gary was sprawled on the sofa reading a book and Sue was playing a computer game.

"Chip is ready for the display," said Mum. "We'll be leaving soon so could you keep an eye on him? I don't want him to get dirty again."

"Don't worry, Mum," answered Sue. "We'll take care of him. He can watch me play this game. Chip likes computer games."

Chip grinned. He did. And he especially liked the one Sue was playing now – *Tornado Versus the Zapmonsters of Snurg.*

14

Tornado was amazing. He was an alien superhero who could do all sorts of stunts – and he could fly! The Zapmonsters were no match for him.

The robodog stared eagerly at the screen.

It would certainly be great to be like Tornado. He would really impress all the dogs in the park. They would be friendly then!

They would gasp at his spins …

… marvel at his kicks …

… and be amazed at his backflips.

"Aaaaah!" Chip's backflip landed him on top of the begonia.

CRASH!

"Chip! What are you doing?" cried
Sue and Gary. "You're supposed to
keep neat and clean."

Sue straightened the robodog's tail
and Gary brushed bits of earth and
pot plant off his back.

"Mum said you've got to stay tidy," said Sue, trying to look stern.

Chip sighed. No one ever told Tornado to stay tidy.

Sue patted him and smiled, then went back to her computer game.

Gary flopped on to the sofa, lost in his book again.

Chip moped around
for a few minutes
then wandered away.

Next door, Mr and Mrs Minted were
just going back inside with Rex.
"Yes," Mr Minted was saying, "Rex
is certainly top dog in town."
"Of course," replied Mrs Minted.
He's won five events
this year already!"

Chip came into the garden just in time to hear Mr Minted say, "Superb! That dog of ours is certainly flying high!"

Chip blinked in surprise and looked up. He didn't know Rex could fly. He'd never seen him do it. Where was he?

Perhaps he was out flying round the park?

Chip frowned.
Tornado could fly.
Rex could fly.
Why couldn't he?

Perhaps if he bounced high enough
he would take off.

It was worth a try.

His springy legs
twanged as he
began bouncing.

With each bounce he went higher
until he could see over the rooftops.

But it was no good. Each time he
went up he came back down again.
He gave it one more try – a *huge*
bounce.

Up and up he went. At the top of
the bounce Chip thrashed his legs
about to try and stay airborne.

But it was useless. All he managed
to do was flip himself over. Down
he came again ...

… and this time he landed in the tree.

"Woo-aaarf!" he barked, startled, as he dropped through the branches.

Twigs snapped and leaves tore loose all around him. Suddenly, he came to a halt. One of his back legs had caught on a branch.

Chip was left dangling helplessly about two metres from the ground.

"Wooo!" he howled.

Gary and Sue heard him and came running out, followed by their dad with a ladder.

"How did you get up there, Chip?" gasped Sue.

"Flying high," replied Chip.

"What do you mean?" said Gary, puzzled.

Then, as Dad lifted the robodog out of the tree, Gary snapped his fingers.

"I know!" he cried. "Chip was watching *Tornado*. I'll bet that's what this is all about."

"Well," said Sue, grinning. "If Chip wants to be a superhero, then I've got just the thing."

27

Sue dashed into the house and came
out a moment later with a small
piece of material.

"It's a cape from an
old Red Riding
Hood doll," she
said, attaching it
to Chip's neck.
Chip beamed. Now not only
did he *look* like a superhero ...

... he *felt*
like one!

Just then Mum arrived.
"Chip!" she groaned. "What have
you been up to?"

Gary and Sue
explained and
Mum looked
anxious.

"Let's hope Chip's motors haven't
overheated," she said and checked
him over again.

"Hmm," she murmured, frowning. "They have. The cooling fan isn't strong enough."

She looked at her watch. "I just have enough time to fit a more powerful one before we go."

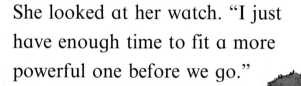

"Come on, Chip," she said and the robodog followed her into the workshop.

A few minutes later they emerged,
Chip wagging his tail.

"The new cooling fan is working
perfectly," said Mum.

"I'm just going indoors
to change. I'll be back
in a moment."

She looked at Sue and Gary.
"Could you remove the cape and
keep an eye on him *this* time?"

Sue and Gary nodded.

"Don't worry, Mum," said Gary.

"Chip will stay right here."

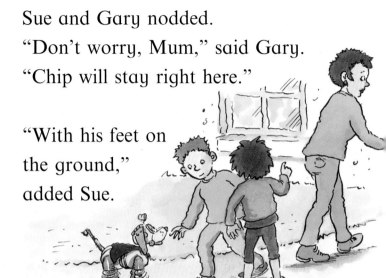

"With his feet on
the ground,"
added Sue.

They sat down on either side of
Chip.

"He won't get into any more
mischief."

"Woof!" barked Chip and Sue laughed.

"You're such a cool dog," she said.

"Yes. Really cool," agreed Gary.

Chip nodded. Of course he was cool. Hadn't he just been fitted with a powerful, new cooling fan?"

He could adjust it himself so he decided to show them just how cool he could be.

Sue and Gary heard a series of
small clicks as the robodog turned
his fan up to maximum.

A great whoosh
of air blasted
out of the grill
in Chip's
underside …

… and to everyone's surprise he shot
straight up into the air.

"Chip!" yelled Sue and Gary as Mum and Dad came rushing out of the house.

The family watched in disbelief as the robodog soared higher and higher until he disappeared from sight.

"The cooling fan!"
groaned Mum.
"It was too
powerful!"

"What will happen to
Chip?" Sue asked
anxiously.

Mum frowned.
"He can control the fan so he
should be able to land without
crashing," she replied.

"We have to find him,"
said Dad. "We'll split
up and meet back here
in half an hour. Come on,
everybody!"

They all dashed off in different
directions but there was one thought
in all of their minds.

What if Chip couldn't control the
fan and had crash-landed already?

But they shouldn't have worried.
Chip was still in the air … and he
was enjoying himself. He had
figured out how
to adjust the
cooling fan so
he could go
up or down.

And he had learned how to spin his
tail to make himself go forward.

Now he was just like Tornado …
and Rex.

He swooped and dived all over the sky.

It felt wonderful to be a superhero.

Suddenly he realized he was over the
park. Looking down he saw that the
dogs were still there.

Now was his chance to impress them
and make friends!

Screaming out of the sky in a power
dive he zoomed over the heads of
the startled dogs.

Then, screeching round in a tight
turn, he rolled over, looped-the-loop
and landed right in front of them.
"Woof!" he barked.

"Owwww!" howled the dogs in fright, turning tail and running for their lives.

Chip couldn't believe it. His only chance of making friends had failed.

What was the point in being a superhero if nobody liked you?

He trudged out of the park just as
Mum came running along the street.
"Chip!" she cried, relieved. "There
you are!"

She took off the cape
and checked the robodog over.

"Thank goodness
you're all right,"
she said,
stroking him.

Chip's head drooped again.
"Oh dear, said Mum. "You don't
look very happy. Shooting into the
air like that must have
scared you."

She looked at her watch.
"Never mind," she
went on.

"We're still in time
for the robot
display. Come on,
that will cheer you
up. I'll phone
home from there."

But there was another disappointment
in store. When they got to the Town
Hall they found that this year's
display had been cancelled.

CANCELLED

Now Mum was unhappy too.
She and Chip trudged home,
feeling very downcast.

Outside the garden gate they met up with Dad, Sue and Gary. They were overjoyed to see Chip again, but sorry about the display.

"What a shame," said Gary. "But never mind, there's always next year."

As they all went through the gate a
sudden, furious barking broke out
from next door. Selina,
the Minteds' cat,
had scratched Rex
on the nose and
he was chasing
her round a tree.

With a yowl,
Selina leapt into
the branches …

... and without thinking Rex hurled himself after her.

The cat swarmed swiftly up into the topmost branches and Rex tried to follow.

Halfway up the tree he realized he had made a terrible mistake.

With a whimper
of fright he
slipped and
began to fall.

Frantically, he wrapped his paws
round a branch and swung into
space.

"Owww!"
he howled.

The branch creaked
and began
to break.
Mr and Mrs
Minted appeared
and stared in
horror.

Dad, who was allergic to dogs,
began to sneeze.
"Ah … ah … ah …
I'll get a ladder,"
he gasped.

CRAAACK!

The branch broke.

"Rexy!" screamed Mrs Minted.

"Rexy!"

Chip suddenly realized that Rex couldn't fly. He had to save him!

Turning his fan up to maximum, the robodog superhero shot upwards ...

... just as Rex came tumbling down.

The falling Afghan landed on Chip's back with a thump.

But Rex was heavy and Chip couldn't stay in the air. With his fan screeching at full power, the robodog was forced back to earth.

He landed heavily with Rex sprawled on top of him.

Shaken, Rex got up.
"Oh, Rexy Wexy! You're safe!
You're all right!"
gushed Mrs Minted,
hugging him.

Worried, the family gathered round
Chip.

"Are you all right,
Chip?" Sue asked
anxiously.

The robodog staggered to his feet and looked up.

"As bright as a button," he croaked and everyone laughed.

"What a cool dog!" exclaimed Gary and Sue.

Mr Minted coughed.

"Er ... we'd just like to say ..." he began.

"Yes," Mrs Minted went on, "we'd just like to say ... thanks to Chip."

The family were startled. The Minteds had never said thanks in their lives.

"He's a brave dog," Mr Minted said
to Mum. "A real dog."

Mum smiled. This more than made
up for missing the robot display.
Rex walked slowly over to Chip. He
had always liked this funny
little dog and now he
wanted to show how
grateful he was.

"Woof," he barked softly and licked
Chip's face. "Woof."

Chip grinned in absolute delight.
"Woof!" he barked back.
"Woof!" returned Rex.

"Woof!" they barked together and
began to race round the garden,
tails wagging.

"They're playing
together!" cried
Sue and Gary.

The robodog barked again with
sheer happiness.

He had found a friend at last.